The Visit

by Bobby Lynn Maslen
pictures by John R. Maslen

Scholastic Inc.
New York • Toronto • London • Auckland • Sydney • Mexico City • New Delhi • Hong Kong • Buenos Aires

Available Bob Books®:

Set 1: Beginning Readers — With consistent new sounds added gradually, your new reader is gently introduced to all the letters of the alphabet. They can soon say, "I read the whole book!®"

Set 2: Advancing Beginners — The use of three-letter words and consistent vowel sounds in slightly longer stories build skill and confidence.

Set 3: Word Families — Consonant blends, endings and a few sight words advance reading skills while the use of word families keep reading manageable.

Set 4: Compound Words — Longer books and complex words engage young readers as proficiency advances.

Set 5: Long Vowels — Silent *e* and other vowel blends build young readers' vocabulary and aptitude.

Bob Books® Collections:

Collection 1 — Includes Set 1: Beginning Readers and part of Set 2: Advancing Beginners

Collection 2 — Includes part of Set 2: Advancing Beginners and Set 3: Word Families

Collection 3 — Includes Set 4: Compound Words and Set 5: Long Vowels

Ask for Bob Books at your local bookstore, or visit www.bobbooks.com.

ISBN 0-545-02711-X

6 5 4 3 2 1   7 8 9 10 11/0

Printed in China
This edition first printing, September 2007

A mouse had a house in
a stone wall.

Toad lived down the hill on the
other side of the road under a rock

Mouse and Toad
were good pals.

Mouse had a white phone. Toad had
a red phone. "Ring-a-ling", rang
Mouse's phone. "Hello, hello", she said.

"Hello, Mouse," said Toad. "I miss
you. I want to go to your
house for a visit."

"Yes, yes," said the mouse. "I will make us a pot of tea." She hung up the phone. She put the teapot on the stove. She set out the cups. She swept the little house

Toad felt happy.
He sang a little tune.
"Off to the mouse house
I will hop. I am so happy I
cannot stop."

He put on his green coat and red slippers. Off Toad went, up the road to Mouse's house.

At last he got to the crossroad.
Toad saw the mouse house
across the road.

But in between, on the busy road were cars, trucks, bikes, motor bikes, and even a bus.

All the drivers were speeding past.
Toot-toot. Honk-honk. Beep-beep."
Stop", said Toad . "Honk-honk",
went the cars.

Soon Toad began to feel bad. He saw the mouse house across the road. "When will I ever see Mouse? When will I have a cup of tea?" he asked.

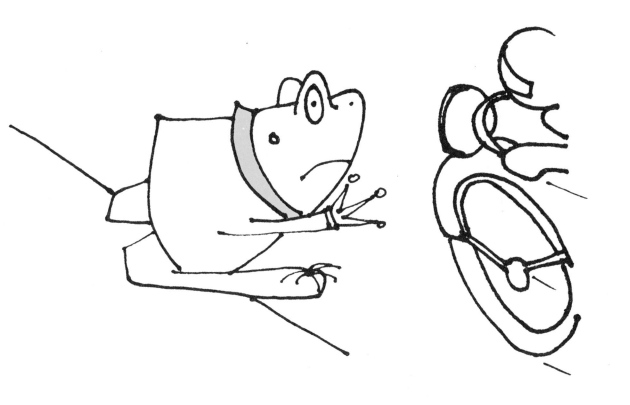

He put a tiny foot into the
street. "Beep-beep", went the
bikes. He jumped back.

Mouse looked out. She saw Toad.
She saw the cars. "Help, help!"
yelled Toad. "I am so unhappy.
I cannot get across the road

Mouse had to stop and think.
"How will I help Toad?" she asked
herself.

All of a sudden she had a good
idea. She took white paint and
a big red card. On one side
she painted "STOP."

On the other side she painted
"Toad Crossing." She went outside
with the bold sign. She waved it up and
down. She turned it from side to side.

The cars stopped. The trucks
stopped. The bikes stopped.
The motor bikes stopped.
Even the bus stopped.

oad looked to the left. He looked
o the right. No wheels were moving
ithin his sight. He walked across the
oad and everything was all right.

"Thank you, Mouse," Toad gratefully said. "No problem", said Mouse, as the two went into the house. "I am always happy to help a toad across the road!

The End

Book 14 contains:

Silent E:

u - e   tune

Long Vowel Combination:

oa   -   toad